Peter Paula
and
the Pelican

by
Brent Cheetham

Grosvenor House
Publishing Limited

The right of Brent Cheetham to be identified as the author of this
work has been asserted in accordance with Section 78
of the Copyright, Designs and Patents Act 1988

The book cover picture is copyright to EacheanE

This book is published by
Grosvenor House Publishing Ltd
28-30 High Street, Guildford, Surrey, GU1 3EL.
www.grosvenorhousepublishing.co.uk

A CIP record for this book
is available from the British Library

ISBN : 978-1-78623-019-5

Peter, Paula
and
the Pelican

"You two are always getting under my feet," said Mrs Brown. "Can't you go out and play in the woods?"

"I don't want to play with Paula, she is just a stupid girl," said Peter about his younger sister."

"Wash your mouth out with soap and water young Peter and don't be so silly."

"But Mum," replied Peter.

"No buts," said Mrs Brown, "and before you go out tuck your shirt in and comb your hair, you look a right mess."

"Nobody is going to see me with my shirt out in the woods so why should I have to tuck it in?" said Peter.

"Because I say so, that's why Peter, and any more silly comments from you cheeky monkey or there will be no peanut butter sandwiches for a month."

"Now run along," said Mrs Brown "and don't forget to be nice and look after your baby sister."

Peter took hold of his sister Paula's hand and almost dragged her towards the door, as Mrs Brown said, "and don't forget to get back before it goes dark, as it's not only me you will have to deal with but your father".

And so it was that morning Peter and Paula went to play in the woods. Not long after leaving their cottage in the village of Sleepy Hollow on the footpath to the woods they came across a hole in the bottom of a hedge.

Peter stopped and said, "let's explore were this hole leads to,"

But Paula said, "No I want to play in the woods".

"What are you scared of?" replied Peter. "Not only are all girls stupid, but they aren't brave like us boys."

At this point he started dragging poor Paula into the hole.

Paula started crying and said, "I don't want to go, I want to play in the woods."

"Don't be a cowardly, cowardly custard, like a silly, stupid girl," said Peter.

Paula stopped crying, as she knew that Peter was bigger than her, and always got his own way. The two of them crawled on their hands and knees in the dark through the tunnel. Peter in the lead. Soon Peter came up to, what looked like a large oak door with a handle. Peter tried to open the door, but it was stuck tight.

Peter said, "there appears to be a door here but it won't open".

"Fine," replied Paula, "let's go back, and go and play in the woods".

"No," retorted Peter. "Come on Paula give us a hand and we can both try and open it."

"But what if there are monsters? Lions or dragons on the other side," said Paula.

"Don't be such a stupid girl; this is England in 1925, not the dark ages. There are no lions, monsters or dragons around today; the last dragon was killed years ago by somebody called St George. Now come on give us a hand."

At this Paula crawled to Peters side and they both started at first to pull and then push the door open.

After some time Peter said, "we will give it one last push," and the door flung open and they both fell on the grass on the other side. But as they did so the door behind closed behind them with a large bang. They both rushed back to the door and try as they might, the door refused to open again.

Paula started crying yet again, and said, "I want to go home."

Perhaps there is another hole in the hedge said Peter, as he ran up and down looking for one. But he could not find one and he nearly burst out crying himself, but stopped himself as he did not want to be seen crying in front of a mere girl.

After some time Peter said, "I wonder where we are, this seems a strange land".

At this Paula said, "Yes Peter just look in the sky there are two suns."

Peter, Paula
and
the Pelican 2

Peter looked up and could not believe his eyes, yes there were two suns high up in the sky. He rubbed his eyes in disbelief. He then spotted a white object in the sky, he could not make out what it was as he pointed to it and said, "What is that?"

But all Paula could say was, "I want to go home now."

The white object was getting bigger and bigger and Peter said it must be a seagull, but as it got closer and he could tell it was too big for a seagull. It was not long before the white object landed next to them in the meadow. Peter could now make out what it was with its giant beak; it was a large white pelican.

The pelican waddled up to our two young children and said, "good morning, have not seen you in these parts before, what are your names?"

Peter being somewhat surprised had his mouth open, so the pelican repeated his request. All Peter could say was, "Well what's your name?"

The Pelican replied. "I asked first, "but my name is The Pelican of course, now what are your names?"

"Oh," said Peter, "I am Peter and this is my baby sister Paula and I have one question for you Mr Pelican."

"Fire away, young man," said the pelican, "what is your question?"

"My question is where we are?"

The pelican replied, "in Back to Front Land, under the rule of the great King Lupin the Second of course, don't you know anything -- are you lost or something?"

"Look Mr Pelican," said Peter. "We have just come from the other side of that hedge, and through that door, but we can't open the door and we want to go home now."

"What," replied the pelican. "No one is allowed the other side of that hedge it's forbidden under the law passed by King Lupin the First."

"Just tell us how we can get home and we will leave you in peace in your Back to Front Land," said Peter.

The pelican said, "well that's simple all you need is the key to the door, you can open it and go home."

There was a gap before Peter spoke yet again, "well are you going to give us the key or show us where it is, as we are both hungry and thirsty and we want to go home."

The pelican said, "only King Lupin has the key to that door, so you will have to ask him."

"I thought you said it was simple," said Peter, "where is the king so we can ask him for the key?"

"Well he lives in a big house in the big city," said the Pelican, "but I doubt if he will see you on account of the Brent of course."

"What is the Brent when he is at home?" replied Peter.

"You don't seem to know anything said the Pelican, "the Brent is a great big ugly giant, with moles on his face, who goes to the big city every now and again and demands peanut butter sandwiches and often knocks off chimney pots and tiles from the roofs city houses just for the hell of it, of course".

"But how will the Brent stop us seeing the king?" said Peter, "and will you stop saying of course at the end of every sentence."

The pelican replied, "Well since the Brent has been terrorising the big city the king has become too afraid to come out of his bedroom, and he says he does not want to meet anybody other than the Prime Minster Mr Herbert Spencer."

Peter, Paula
and
the Pelican 3

"Oh," replied Peter. "But we must see the Prime Minister, he may be able to help." –

The pelican put one wing to his chin, in a thoughtful look – and said, "I don't see why not, he seems a nice sort of a chap, I will take you to the big city, you two can fly can't you?"

Paula was just about to speak, when Peter said, "of course we can," and started running around the pelican, flapping his arms up and down. Round and round the pelican he went. Flap, flap, flapping his arms as if they were wings. Peter then started run to a figure of eight, between the pelican and Paula, shouting, "I can fly, I can fly," whilst still flapping his arms up and down.

Paula was not impressed and pulled a stern face and shouted out to Peter, "Don't be silly, we can't fly, only birds can fly."

Peter said, "Oh shut up you are just a stupid girl, and girls don't know how to have fun."

The pelican held one wing up to stop Peter running, and said to Peter, "Can you or can you not fly, is your sister telling the truth?" Peter looked stumped for once and had to admit that Paula was right, as indeed they could not fly.

"Can you walk?" said the Pelican.

"Well yes." said Peter.

"Good," said the pelican. "Follow me, and we will all walk to the big city together."

And so it was that Peter, Paula and the pelican started their long walk to the big city.

"Can you tell us something about this kingdom of Back to Front Land?" asked Peter.

"Since you don't know a thing I suppose I tell you a little about us," said the pelican. "But there is not much to tell, King Lupin rules over us, and all the work on the land is done by the happy monkeys which live in the forest by night and by day they run our farms. We have to pay them peanuts for all the hard work they do. We would be lost without them," said the pelican "All the able bodied men over the age of 18, work down the peanut butter mines and peanut butter is this kingdom's one and only export."

The pelican took a breath and went on, "of course we only mine peanuts from the peanut butter mines, and we have to mix it with butter, which the monkeys make in giant tanks to make the peanut butter."

"Oh I just love peanut butter sandwiches," said Peter. "Yum Yum, I am growing to like this place more by the minute."

After walking for what seemed an age they came across a row of chickens sitting on the top of a brick wall all talking at the same time. But the strange thing about them was that they were all knitting with brightly coloured wool.

"Good Morning ladies," said the pelican "And how are you this bright and fine day?"

"Oh we are busy as usual, hard at work knitting, a chicken's work is never done." –

"What are they knitting?" Paula asked the pelican.

"Egg cosies of course," replied the Pelican.

"Can I have a look at one?" said Paula.

At this the largest and oldest old mother hen, proudly gave Paula, an egg cosy to look at.

"These egg cosies look strange," said Paula, "they are all out of shape, in fact they look square."

"Well of course they are square," said the pelican. Why would they be anything but square?"

Peter, Paula and the Pelican 4

"An egg cosy should be round," said Paula, "Everybody should know that – round egg cosies for round eggs." —

At this the chickens started to laugh, "Why would any chicken want to lay a round egg? – A round egg that's stupid, what good are round eggs?" and one chicken started up – "why how silly is that, round eggs would have to have special boxes, with round holes to carry them in, and think how could folks store them in their larders, you couldn't stack them up, they would just fall out onto the floor and break."

"Yes,' said another chicken, falling about laughing, "Just imagine if you put a round egg on a table, it would just roll off, on to the floor and crack open leaving a mess. Whoever heard of a round egg, we only lay square eggs here."

Old Mother hen looked Paula in the face and said, "I don't know where you come from but you appear to live in some sort of back to front country – You should go and tell your chickens to start laying square eggs, I am sure they would be happy to do so."

Paula just scratched her head, whilst Peter for once just stood still, with his hands on his hips saying nothing.

The pelican just said, "you must come from, a very silly land, an out of date place, if your hens only lay round eggs."

All both Peter and Paula could do is nod in agreement.

"Well it's been nice talking to you, we must be on our way," said Paula "and thanks for the advice, I will have a word with the hens when I get back and ask them to lay square eggs."

At this the hens all waved them goodbye, with their small dumpy wings, as they all said, "have a nice journey, hope to see you again sometime."

All three continued their walk towards the big city and Paula said, "What a nice bunch of hens they all were."

Peter just shrugged his shoulders in a form of acknowledgement. After a while they came across a tractor in a field being driven by a monkey. The tractor stopped dead, in a puff of smoke, beside them. The monkey looked at them and said, "dam thing keeps on breaking down it's about time King Lupin the Second, brought us all new tractors."

"Can we be of any help?" asked the pelican.

"Perhaps you can said the monkey, there is a tool box at the back of the tractor, and perhaps you could pass me my tools whilst I try and fix the engine."

The monkey opened up the sides of the engine and started doing something to the engine. He said, "Could someone pass me the monkey wrench and a monkey spanner?" and at this Peter reached into the toll box and passed the two items on to the monkey.

"Thanks," Replied the monkey, this should do fine. Shortly latter the Monkey said, "I think I will need a hammer, is there a monkey hammer in that box you could pass me?"

Peter made a fumble about in the toolbox, and after some time produced a hammer, which he duly passed up to the monkey.

The monkey said, "Thanks this should do the trick, and begin banging at something on the engine. The monkey went back to the driver's seat and asked Peter to turn a handle at the front of the tractor.

"Crossed fingers said the monkey, "let's hope she starts. Ok start turning the handle now," said the monkey.

Peter turned the handle and with yet another puff of smoke the tractor came back into life.

Peter, Paula
and
the Pelican 5

The monkey shouted over the noise of the engine "Where are you all going?"

Peter replied, "we are off to see the Prime Minster, I forget his name," at which point Paula interjected and said, "I remember its Herbert Spencer."

Peter continued, "As I was saying we are off to see the Prime Minister Herbert Spencer to try and get an audience with the king, as we need the key to the door in the hedge back there in order to go home."

The monkey said, "I wish you the best of luck, keep going on this path until you meet the silly sheep, and a word of warning about the sheep, they always have a problem, as they never tell lies, but always tell the truth."

"Telling the truth is a problem?" said Peter.

"It can be," said the monkey, "so watch what you say, any way best of luck and have a safe journey."

The monkey drove off in his tractor, and Peter, Paula and the pelican continued their long walk to the big city. After a while Paula said, "My feet hurt and they are sore, I am hot and thirsty and hungry, when are we going to have something to eat and drink?"

"Stop moaning," said Peter, "just typical of all stupid girls, all day long, all they do is moan, moan, moan."

The pelican, said "don't you know that in Back to Front Land, if you wish for something that is reasonable and you are not greedy your wish will be granted."

"Well I wish for a drink of water and a sandwich," said Paula.

And as Paula finished the sentence there appeared in front of them a sign saying free food and drink for all weary travellers and beside the sign was an empty table with a tablecloth draped over the side, and the tablecloth had a happy smiley face on it. To their amazement the tablecloth spoke, "good day to you folks and what can I do for you today, hungry and thirsty are we?"

"Yes we are," said Peter, "we are very, very thirsty and hungry.

"Not a problem," said the table cloth, "now Mr Pelican you first what to you fancy?"

The pelican just said one word, "fish," and ping a large live fish appeared on the table. The pelican just grabbed the fish in its giant beak and swallowed it down whole.

"Now how about you two children what do you want?"

Peter said, "Peanut butter sandwiches and ginger beer."

Ping – lo and behold two peanut butter sandwiches and two glasses of ginger beer appeared on the table before them.t

The tablecloth said, "enjoy, but be warned you are only allowed one sandwich and one glass of ginger beer each."

But Peter was not really listening to the tablecloth and just grabbed the peanut butter sandwich off the plate and stuffed it into his mouth and when he had finished it gulped down the glass of ginger beer all in one, whist Paula took her time eating and drinking. As soon as Peter had replaced the plate and the glass on the table, then Ping —they were replaced by another peanut butter sandwich and another glass of ginger ale.

Peter, Paula
and
the Pelican 6

No sooner had they appeared then Peter made a grab for the peanut butter sandwich and Paula shouted, "No don't eat it.

But predictably Peter said, "Oh shut up your just a stupid girl, you know nothing."

Peter took one giant bite out of the sandwich and then spat it out.

"It tastes of mud," he proclaimed, and as he did so he picked up the glass of ginger ale to wash away the taste of the mud. He poured the glass down his throat, but as it hit his lips it turned to sand.

"Yuk," he said spitting sand out all over the pelican.

"That will teach you," said Paula. "Did you not hear the pelican say you are not to be greedy and the tablecloth said we are only allowed one sandwich and one glass of ginger beer each?"

But Peter was not listening and was too busy spitting mud and sand out of his mouth.

After what seemed an age the Pelican said, "It's time to make a move on or we will never get to see the Prime Minster or the King today,

"They continued on their journey, with Peter every now and again, still spitting out the remains of his last sandwich and drink until they came to a sign saying "Peanut Butter Mines this way: – They stopped and looked at the peanut butter mine, and saw peanuts being placed from bags marked "Peanuts" into giant tanks by the peanut butter miners, whilst monkeys were pouring in the butter, and stirring it with large ladles. At the bottom of the tank was a tap, and another monkey was turning it on and off, and filling up jars with peanut butter. One of the monkeys waved at them and Peter and Paula waved back.

"Come on you two," said the pelican, "can't stand around all day gawping, it's time we got a move on" and it was not long before they came to T-junction where on the grass was a sheep eating some grass."

"That must be the silly sheep," said Peter.

The pelican replied, "Yes I think you must be right".

When they got to the T-junction they noticed a sign pointing one to the right and one to the left, but both saying, "This way to the Big City".

Peter scratched his head and said, "which way should we go? Which way is best, and if as in answer to his own question said, "I know I will ask the silly sheep, he may be silly but at least honest. "Good day to you Mr Sheep, are you known as the silly sheep?" said Peter

"Yes I am" replied the sheep. "We may be silly, but I am known as an honest sheep in these here parts".

"I wonder if you could help us – can you tell us which way it is to the big city, the sign doesn't appear to be much help."

"Well said the sheep just follow the sign." –

Peter said, "The sign is nearly as silly as you as it points in two opposite directions, both saying to the big city".

"The sheep sighed and just looked at Peter and said, "just follow the sign, it's that simple."

Peter raised his eyes to the sky, and after a moment brought them back down on the pelican.

"One last try," he said. "Now look Mr Silly Sheep, which is the shortest way to the big city?" "Ah," said the silly sheep, "that's easy, why did you not ask me that in the first place? It's to the right".

"Thank you Mr Silly sheep, now I know why they call you silly".

Peter, Paula and the Pelican 7

Once again the pelican led the way, followed by Peter with Paula bringing up the rear.

"How much further and how much longer will it be before we reach the big city?" said Paula.

"No idea said Peter, "and do try and keep up, I know you are only a girl, but do you best ".

The pelican said, "at a guess I would say we are about half way there."

Soon the path got narrower and narrower, and muddier and muddier, trees, stinging nettles and brambles began to close in on them. "I don't like this cried Paula I don't want to go on."

Peter turned round to Paula and pointed his finger at her, "you stupid girl, we have got no choice, so stop you moaning and just keep walking."

Soon the brambles and stinging nettles began to hurt, and the brambles caught on the clothing, and even made small scratch marks on Peter and Paula's legs and arms, whilst the pelican had to stop every now and again to free himself from the weeds. Next they found they were climbing a steep hill, but still with vegetation on both sides.

"Are you sure we are on the right path, and are we going the right way," said Paula.

"Of course we are said Peter, the silly sheep never tells a lie remember."

After a further hour, they reached the top of the hill, all puffed out. The pelican looked to where the path led next. Peter and Paula just sat down to take a breath of fresh air.

The pelican said, "I have some good news for you, the path that leads down this side of this hill has no vegetation, its dry, but a very steep path, You may have to slide down most of the way on your hands and feet. You can see where the path ends down by that post, with what looks like some bird perched on it. No use me walking down with you two, I will just fly to the bottom, see you two soon," and as soon as the pelican finished the sentence he took a running jump off the side of the hill and flew away.

"Better get a move on," said Peter as they both got up and viewed the steep path down. Soon they were sliding using hands and feet, and on occasions on their bottoms. It did not take time for to them to reach the end of the path and to meet the pelican again, who was standing next to an owl wearing glasses who was reading a book on top of a post.

"Good day to you all," said the owl. "I wonder if I can be of any help in your travels."

Peter looked at the owl, and said, "Its day time, owls only come out at night, what are you doing perched on that post at midday."

"Ah," said the owl, "good question, well you have heard of the night owl, well I am the day owl. You might well ask me why I am the day owl. Well see these glasses I am reading with? I have bad eyesight – I was a night owl once, but what with my bad eyesight, I just kept on bumping into things in the half-light and doing myself an injury. Can't have an owl crashing into trees and disturbing the peace on the woods can we? That's why I decided to become the day owl.

"Oh sorry to hear about your poor eyesight," said Peter, "but perhaps you could help us get to the big city as we have to see Prime Minister".

Paula interjected, "Herbert Spencer".

"Yes, I know Herbert Spencer, to help us go home to our nice cottage in Sleepy Hollow," said Peter.

Peter, Paula
and
the Pelican 8

The day owl slowly took off his spectacles, with his left wing, and with his right wing produced a white handkerchief from under his wing, and then proceeded to wipe his glasses clean.

"Hold your horses children," said the day owl. "First of all we have not been introduced and why do you want to see the Prime Minister?"

"Oh," said the pelican, "this is Peter and his baby sister Paula, and they need to see the Prime Minister in order to see King Lupin, so that the can get the key to the door that leads to the outside world".

"Interesting," said the day owl, "and before we move on why did you take that path, over the forest and the hill to get here, when you could have gone round the hill in half the time? You have not been speaking to the silly sheep have you and have asked the wrong question?"

"Peter just scratched his head."

But Paula said, "ah, I think I know what you mean Mr day owl, Peter asked the silly sheep, which path was the shortest path, and the sheep being honest give us the shortest path, however the shortest path is not the best path. What Peter should have asked is which path is the quickest path or the best path, am I right Mr day owl"

"My, My you have got a bright sister," said the Day owl. Peter just stood there and frowned.

The day owl turn half round on his post and pointed with his wing to a small building in the distance and said, "Your best option is to go straight to that small shed in the distance, where the monkey's keep the retired nonsense horse, he will take you all the way to the big city.

"Why do you call him the nonsense horse Mr Day Owl?" said Peter

Paula by this time was getting brave and said, "is it because the horse just talks nonsense Mr Day Owl?"

"Right yet again Paula, "said the day owl, "your sister, is quick off the mark yet again."

This bought about an even bigger frown from Peter.

"Well we must be on our way now Mr Day Owl," said the pelican and soon all three found themselves at the small shed and in that shed they found an old horse with his head down eating out of a bucket.

"Good morning," said the pelican to the horse, "are you the nonsense horse?"

"Nonsense horse, nonsense horse what complete and utter nonsense my name is Brian," replied the horse.

"Excuse me whilst I finish this delicious Back to Front Land carrot soup," said Brian the horse. "Smells nice," said Paula, "what is in the carrot soup Brian, have you got the recipe?"

Brian replied, "What's in it? Carrots and soup of course,"

Peter nudged Paula, and said, "I think this must be the nonsense horse all right."

Brian the horse finished his soup. He looked up at all three and said, "It's a nice day; I saw it on the radio this morning!"

Pete said, "how you can see something on the radio Brian?"

"Simple," replied Brian, the monkeys turned on the radio, and I saw it."

At that point a small mouse ran across the stable floor, and Brian said to Peter, "Would that be the same mouse I saw yesterday?"

Peter said, "I don't know".

"Not very clever then are you?" said Brian the horse.

Peter, Paula
and
the Pelican 9

The pelican then said to Brian the nonsense horse, "We have just been told by the day owl, you can take us to the big city, could you do that for us?"

"My pleasure, said Brian.

Peter said, "Ah there's life in the old horse yet".

"Old horse, old horse," replied Brian. "I will have you know I am only aged two, and as fit as a fiddle".

And at this Brian proceeded to do a dance in the stable, but after about 30 seconds his legs got crossed and he almost fell over, puffed out. Peter just raised his eyes to the stable roof, whilst, Paula and the pelican just laughed.

Brian, said after he regained his breath, "Just climb up on my back and I will take you to the big city, and the pelican can ride on my head, pull up that chair in the corner that will help you two children climb up and we will be off". Soon Peter, Paula, the Pelican, and Brian the nonsense horse were on the road again.

After a while Brian started talking nonsense, "why is the sea so wet?" he said.

"Don't know, "replied Peter.

"So that the fish can go for a walk," said Brian.

Peter said, "That's not funny, that's just daft and silly".

Paula laughed and said, "I think that's funny, don't you know how to have fun Peter, I just love Brian, the nonsense horse, so carry on Brian," as she give him a pat on the side.

"Why are there clouds in the sky?" said Brian

"Don't know," said Paula

"Because if they were not in the sky, they would be on the ground, and they would not be clouds at all but fog".

Paula burst out laughing saying, "There is some sense in what you say," whilst Peter just sat there with a glum face.

Brian then went into a little rhyme, "I don't, like tea, I don't like water, perhaps I oughta".

"Don't think I can stand much more of this," said Peter.

Both Paula and the pelican said in unison, "Oh do shut up Peter".

Brian continued with his nonsense talk, "roses are reddish, grass are greenish, but why is horseradish not horse colour? Ha ha".

Soon they came in sight of the big city, and they saw the county's flag flying from a big house in the centre of town. The flag was red, white and blue, with a large jar of peanut butter jar in the centre. The pelican pointed to the flag with one wing and said that's where King Lupin and the Prime Minster Herbert Spencer live. Soon they were in the market square, in the centre of which was a giant table, with ladders on all sides leading up to the top.

After dismounting Brian the nonsense horse and telling him he could go home, all three marched up to the big house with a big door, and knocked hard on the big knocker.

Soon the door opened and a man in a black top hat and black suit opened the door and said, "I am Herbert Spencer the Prime Minister how can we help you folks today?"

"We have come to see King Lupin, about getting the key to the door in the hedge to the outside world," said Peter.

"Oh," said the prime minster, "I don't think the king, will see you, as he is too scared to come out of his bedroom, he will only see me, and perhaps anybody who can help deal with the BRENT problem".

Peter replied, "I don't think..."

But before he could go on Paula nudged peter in the stomach and said; "we don't think that's a problem, we just maybe able to help King Lupin with the Brent problem".

"Well if that's the case come on in," said the Prime Minster, and soon they were going up a flight of narrow stairs that leads to the King's bedroom.

Peter, Paula
and
the pelican 10

The Prime Minster knocked on the Kings door, "Who is it?" came from within.

"It's Herbert Spencer," replied the Prime Minster.

"Do come in," was the faint reply from the bedroom.

The Prime Minister went in first followed by Peter, Paula and the pelican. King Lupin was standing by his bed in his nightgown and his crown. The Prime Minister bowed to the King and said, "Your majesty I have brought these children and a pelican to see you".

As soon as the king saw the children the king went all red, and jumped into bed, with just his crown showing above the sheets.

King Lupin shouted from under the bed sheets, "why have you brought these children here? I said I only wanted to see you, are they going to hurt me? You're a very, very bad Prime Minister to disobey my instructions.

"Sorry your majesty," said the Prime Minster, "but they might be able to help us with the Brent problem, and they need the key to the door in the hedge in order to go home".

"Well tell them they can't have the key unless they sort out the Brent problem. If they can't sort out the Brent problem, they will just have to stay here forever and ever".

No sooner had the king finished his little speech, then church bells started ringing, "Oh no, the Brent is back," said the Prime Minster as he ran to the window followed yet again by Peter, Paula and the pelican. The Prime Minster pointed to the giant table, and Peter, Paula and the pelican noticed folks rushing up and down the ladders to the tabletop.

"If the people cannot get enough fresh peanut sandwiches to that table top before the Brent comes he goes mad, and knocks of more chimney pots and roof tiles than he normally does...Faster, faster," urged the Prime Minster to the folks running up and down the ladders, although of course they could not hear him.

Then they all heard a crashing sound in the distance, which must have been the Brent knocking off a chimney pot, followed by a deep loud voice saying, "I want my peanut butter sandwiches and I want them NOW".

Then all of a sudden Paula, ran out of the room and down the steps. Everybody in the room was dismayed, but no one wanted to follow her. The Brent appeared in the market square and growled, then started to pick up the peanut butter sandwiches and eat them one at a time. By this time all the folks had retreated to their house and were hiding behind closed curtains. What came next, folks could not believe their eyes, as Paula ran into the market square and kicked the BRENT in the leg and the shin.

"Ouch," said the Brent, "What do you want to do that for? That hurts "

But Paula just kicked the Brent yet again and said, "you're a nasty brute and a beastly man, why do you want to scare all these innocent people you horrible man?"

The Brent bent down and picked Paula up in his hand. "Now look here little girl, I am not horrible," said the Brent

"Oh yes you are, you knock their chimney pots off and scare the life out of them, so why do you do that?"

The Brent had a tear in his eye and looked Paula in the eye and said, "an eye for an eye a tooth for a tooth that's what I say".

Peter, Paula
and
the Pelican 11

Paula replied, "sorry I am not with you...what do you mean?"

"Well I am an orphan, both my parents died when I was very young. My dad was a peanut butter miner, and slipped and fell into a mixing tank of peanuts and butter and drowned, whilst my mother died after opening a cupboard and a large jar of peanut butter fell on her head. They then sent me away to live with my wicked aunt Miss Grimalkin, who used to beat me. Miss Grimalkin was one nasty woman, and often used to feed me with cat food left on a plate on the floor."

"This story you are telling me about Miss Grimalkin is all very sad and she must have been an evil woman," said Paula, "but it still does not explain why you terrorise the inhabitants of the big city">

"Well my wicked aunt Miss Grimalkin used to tell the neighbours that I was a freak, that I was ugly and was a burden and she only looked after me out of the goodness of her heart. I was a big baby and just kept on growing and by aged 10 I was six foot tall and still growing. Miss Grimalkin said I must have had very stupid parents to die, from falling into a peanut butter tank, and to die from a jar of peanut butter falling on my mum's head, when I was aged four. All the towns' folk used to call me an ugly bug and a freak, and Miss Grimalkin used to give tomatoes to the town's children to throw at me. By the time I reached six foot four inches in height I decided to leave this city, and get my revenge of the towns folk."

"Well I don't think you are ugly," said Paula, "in fact you are quite cute."

At this the Brent had a red flush and said, "nobody has ever said that to me before."

Paula said, "Do you trust me, as I have a plan, but you must agree to do everything I say?"

"I trust you," said the Brent, "but what is your plan?"

"Just stand there and don't say or do a thing until I ask you, now just put me down on the table top."

The Brent placed her on the tabletop...Paula stood still and then shouted, "citizens of the big city you can all come out now, the Brent will not hurt you". She repeated her demand three times, and at last one door opened and two elderly folk came out, a man and his wife. Slowly but surely other doors began to open and other residents came out of their houses. After a while there was a large crowd all standing outside and talking to each other in low voices.

Then Paula shouted out, "and that includes you King Lupin, come out now so that we can all see you".

Everybody looked to the big house but nothing happened, no door opened, the balcony was empty and not a sound came from within.

"Come on King Lupin," said Paula, "are you a man or a mouse, let's see you."

At this the crowd started shouting, "We want the king, we want King Lupin, we want the king, we want King Lupin". The crowd began to shout even louder and at long last the King emerged from the big house on to the balcony, followed, by Herbert Spencer the Prime Minister and Paula's Brother Peter and the pelican. King Lupin stood still and gave a nervous wave to the crowd and the crowd responded by shouting, "God save the king, god save the king".

Paula, waved her hand in the air and shouted, "Good folk of the big city, you all want to solve the Brent problem don't you?"

"Yes we do, yes we do," was the reply.

Peter, Paula
and
the Pelican 12

Paula continued, "now the Brent tells me that when he was small (laughter heard in the crowd) you folks used to be nasty to him and call him names and worst of all sometimes pelt him with tomatoes. Is the right?"

No one spoke...so she said, "is that right?" yet again, and some folk nodded in agreement. "I want to hear you all say yes that's right, come on now folks it's a shame you did this in the first place, but it's even more of a shame you can't admit it. It takes a real human being to admit a mistake".

Someone from the crowd shouted out, "we will admit it only if he says sorry for knocking off our chimney first."

Paula looked down and said, "Since the Brent was the one folks were being nasty to, it's only fair that the folks who did wrong say sorry first. The Brent will say sorry as soon as you apologize for the past. OK shouted another person let's all say sorry provided he says sorry, and promises not to knock off any more chimney pots or roof tiles. It's a deal," shouted Paula.

Paula said, "right after me say sorry for being so cruel to the Brent in the past, one, two, three, go,"

And the whole crowd said, "sorry for being so cruel to the Brent in the past Now your turn Paula said to the Brent".

The Brent said, "Sorry I should not have knocked off your chimney pots and scared you all, I promise not to do so in the future, provided you are nice to me and I get my peanut butter sandwiches."

Hurrah shouted the crowd and King Lupin the second held up his hand and everything went quiet. King Lupin cleared his throat with a small cough and spoke to the crowd, "today is a great day in the history of Back to Front Land, I proclaim today as a holiday and a feast day. Today all my subjects will be able to feast on royal peanut butter sandwiches and royal ginger beer from the royal cellars. The Banquet will be held at the royal parade ground this afternoon, and it will be free to all."

King Lupin turned to the Prime Minster and said, "get off a telegram to the four corners of my kingdom requesting my subject's presence at the royal banquet. This afternoon."

"Hip, hip hooray for the King," the crowd shouted and the King shouted, "Hip, Hip, Hooray for the Brent." . . . And everybody shouted Hip hip hooray for the Brent.

Two hours later Peter, Paula and the pelican were seated at the top table, with King Lupin the Second and Herbert Spencer the Prime Minster. By this time all their old friends had turned up, the monkeys, the peanut butter miners, the chickens (still knitting and laying square eggs), the day owl and the silly sheep, but this time a whole flock of them. Last to turn up was the Brian the nonsense horse, who was driving everybody mad with his nonsense. Peter was busy stuffing his face with peanut butter sandwiches and gulping back glasses of ginger beer.

Paula looked up, and said to Peter, "it's getting late, look the two suns are going down, and we need to get back before dark, mother and father will be worried sick about us, and I can't see how we can get back before it gets dark".

King Lupin overheard what Paula said — and said, "I think we can help you out here. Call for the royal aircraft to come out of the royal hanger and send for the royal pilot. And oh before I forget here is the key to the door in the hedge, you will need that to get back home".

The pelican said, "that aircraft is faster than me, I must leave now and get a head start, so I will see you two children in the meadow by the hedge with the door". At this he got up from the table, across the grass and took to the air.

Peter, Paula and the Pelican 13

The plane, which was a biplane made of wood and canvas, was rolled out of the hanger. It had the royal flag of red, white and blue with the peanut butter jar on its tail. And it had a registration mark P-Nut emblazoned on its wing. King Lupin said it should not be long now, they will just refuel the plane and then you are off home. After half an hour, they still had not been told that it was ready for take-off and both Peter and Paula began to become pensive. Then they spotted the pilot in a leather flying jacket and goggles running towards them. The pilot, who boasted a fine pencil moustache, approached the King.

"Your majesty," he said, "we have a problem, the plane appears to have become stuck down on some muddy wet ground, and we can't seem to move it."

At this Peter started to cry saying, "We will never get home tonight and dad will kill us when we get back".

Paula was thinking and all of a sudden said, "I have got it, why don't we ask the Brent to move the aircraft, he has the strength of ten horses".

The Brent was playing with the children in the field at the time. King Lupin then said to the pilot, "go and ask the Brent for help".

"Will do your majesty," was the reply.

They all observed the pilot and the Brent walking over to the plane, and the Brent pulling the plane out of the mud with little or no effort. Brent gave the thumbs up to the King, and the King said, "it's time for you two to make a move".

So it was that Peter and, Paula, followed by the King and the Prime Minister walked over to the plane. They had laid on a red carpet for Peter and Paula; they indeed were being treated like royalty. The plane started up and began to taxi towards the end of the runway, whilst the Brent shouted to Peter and Paula, "do come back and visit us one day".

The King said, "do come back, my Kingdom will always welcome you with a right royal feast".

Soon they were up in the air, and they noticed that everybody from Back to Front Land was waving at them, so they waved back. Peter then got the hiccups from drinking too much ginger beer, and every time he hiccupped the plane hiccupped with him. This only made Paula laugh, and Peter said it was no laughing matter, which only made Paula laugh all the more.

Next thing after the short flight, they found themselves taxing up to the pelican in the meadow. The engine stopped and Peter and Paula got out.

The pelican said, "you took your time, thought you had got lost for a moment".

"Can't talk now, we must get home. Nice knowing you, said Peter who turned to Paula and said, "You have got the key let us get a move on".

The pelican said, "Its been great fun today, the best day of my life, and since you are such nice children I will continue to look over you, to make sure you are alright".

But by this time Peter, and Paula had opened the door and did not reply to the pelican's comments.

Paula just threw the key back to the pelican saying, "Catch! There is your key back, see you around some time maybe".

The just got back before dusk, and Mr Brown had just returned from work and was talking to Mrs Brown in the Kitchen.

Peter was all exited, "you never guess what," he said, "today we meet a pelican, some talking monkeys, a king, some chickens that lay square eggs and..."

"Hold it there my son," said Mr Brown, "what nonsense you talk. Children and their imagination," he said to Mrs Brown.

Peter, Paula
and the
Pelican 14

Paula said nothing and Mrs Brown said, "what do you two want for tea, peanut butter sandwiches?"

Peter said, "No thanks mum not sure I could face another peanut butter sandwich".

"But they are your favourites," said mum, "Are you feeling all right. Or are you ill?"

"No mum," said Peter "I just want a glass of water then I will go to bed".

Paula said, "I am sure he will be alright in the morning, but I could do with a small jam sandwich before I go to bed".

Mrs Brown made Paula the jam sandwich, after which Paula said, "thank you very much, I will go to bed now, good night mum and good night dad".

"Don't forget our bedtime kisses," said Mr Brown and Paula ran up to Mr Brown and kissed him, and then did the same to Mrs Brown, "good night again," she said

Mr Brown looked out the window and said to Mrs Brown what a lovely sunset, the sky's all red. Mrs Brown held his hand as they both looked out the window. They then spotted a white bird fly past in the half-light. Mr Brown looked at it and said, "That looks like a Pelican".

The End

Lightning Source UK Ltd.
Milton Keynes UK
UKHW010706181121
394190UK00002B/318

9 781786 230195